K'tonton's
Yom Kippur
Kitten

K'tonton's

Yom Kippur

The Jewish Publication Society

Philadelphia and Jerusalem

5755 / 1995

Kitten

Sadie Rose Weilerstein

illustrated by Joe Boddy

In loving memory of Judy

Text copyright © 1995 by Sadie Rose Weilerstein
Illustrations copyright © 1995 by Joe Boddy
Jacket illustration copyright © 1995 by Joe Boddy

Manufactured in the United States of America
Library of Congress Cataloging-in-Publication Data

Weilerstein, Sadie Rose, 1894–1994
K'tonton's Yom Kippur kitten / Sadie Rose Weilerstein; illustrated by Joe Boddy.
p. cm.
Summary: After allowing a small kitten to take the blame for something he did, K'tonton, a thumb-sized young boy, feels guilty when he goes to services at the synagogue on Yom Kippur.
ISBN 0–8276–0541–2
[1. Jews—Fiction. 2. Yom Kippur—Fiction. 3. Fasts and feasts–Judaism—Fiction. 4. Cats—Fiction.] I. Boddy, Joe, ill.
II. Title.
PZ7.W435Ky.   1955
[E]—dc20   95–8541
                                                    CIP
                                                    AC

10   9   8   7   6   5   4   3   2

Jacket and text design by Susan Hermansen

Once upon a time a mischievous little boy was born. He had black eyes and black hair, dimples in his knees, and thumbs just right for sucking. There was only one thing odd about him: He was exactly the size of a thumb, not one bit smaller or larger. And because he was so small, his parents called him *K'tonton,* which means very, very small.

Over the years K'tonton grew until he was as tall as his father's middle finger. By this time he wasn't a baby any longer. He wore pants and a shirt and was a busy little chatterbox, dancing around on tables and chairs, peeping into boxes, and hiding behind bowls, asking questions—so many questions—and always finding his way into another adventure. . . .

It all began the day after Rosh Hashanah, the Jewish New Year. K'tonton and his mother were in the kitchen.

Meow, meow! came a faint sound.

A thin little gray-and-white kitten stood in the doorway. No one knew whose kitten it was or where it had come from. K'tonton didn't know. His father didn't know. His mother didn't know! It looked at K'tonton and mewed pitifully.

"It's hungry," said K'tonton. "Give it some milk, please, Mother."

But Mother shook her head.

"If I give it milk, it will come back every day."

Just the same, she filled a saucer with milk and set it down in the doorway.

Lap, lap, lap! In and out, in and out went the kitten's pink tongue until the saucer was empty.

The very next day the kitten came back, just as
Mother had said it would. On the third day it came,
too. Mother was busy making *taiglach*, delicious honey
pastries. She set a cup of honey at the edge of the table
and got the kitten its dish of milk. Father called her at
that moment.

In and out, in and out, went the kitten's pink tongue. K'tonton watched her from his place on the table. It made him hungry to see her lap the milk so greedily. His eyes caught a trickle of honey running

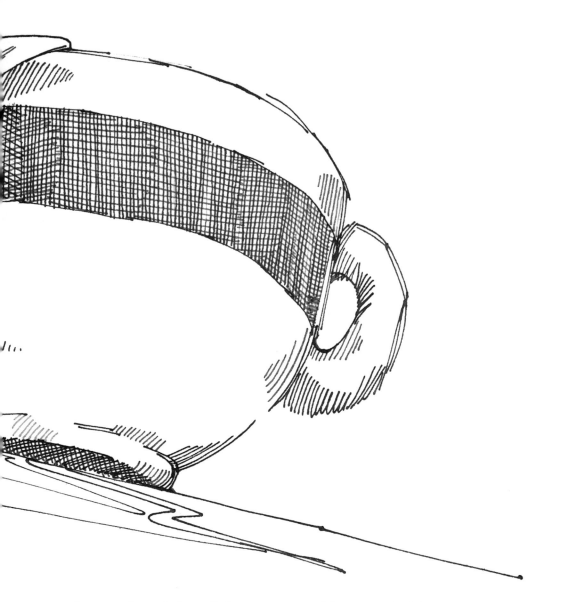

down the side of the cup, and he stuck his finger into
the golden trickle and licked it off. *M-m-m!* It was
good. And there was more honey around the rim of the
cup. K'tonton leaned forward to reach it, when—

CRASH!—down went the cup off the table. The honey ran in a stream across the floor. The startled kitten sprang up and ran through the stream of honey to the door.

Just then, in came Mother.

"Oh, no!" she cried. "My honey! And it's all I have in the house. K'tonton, did you do this?"

K'tonton said nothing.

Mother's eyes found the kitten's sticky footprints on the floor.

"It's that kitten!" she said. "It must have jumped on the table and knocked the cup down. I told you I should never have given it milk."

She looked sternly at K'tonton as if she suspected him of protecting the kitten from being punished.

K'tonton's heart beat wildly.

Speak up, K'tonton, something was whispering inside him. *Tell Mother you knocked the cup over. Don't let the poor kitten take the blame.*

But K'tonton did not speak up. He just stood there looking down at his feet.

The next day, when the kitten came for its milk, Mother shooed it away.

"Scat!" she said. "Scat! No more mischief!"

Oh, how guilty K'tonton felt! But by that time it was even harder to explain than the day before.

Soon it would be Yom Kippur, the Day of Judgment, and K'tonton had this sin on his heart.

"Even the fish in the sea tremble on Yom Kippur," thought K'tonton. "How much more should I be trembling."

"I'll give all my pennies to charity," he said. "I won't keep even one. I'll fast all day, and I'll pray. God will know I am sorry. No one could be more sorry than I am."

He was thinking of the verse in the prayer book, "Charity, prayer, and repentance avert the evil decree."

But there was something else the Torah teaches that K'tonton was trying hard not to think about.

"If you wrong your neighbor, you must go to your neighbor and right the wrong. Otherwise, Yom Kippur cannot atone for you."

K'tonton pushed the thought aside.

At *Minha*—the afternoon service before *Kol Nidrei*—he dropped a coin in every saucer that had been set out in the doorway of the synagogue; a coin for Israel, one for the *yeshivot,* one for the aged, one for the hungry, one for the orphans.

The kitten is hungry without its milk, the voice inside K'tonton whispered. *Maybe it's an orphan, too.*

K'tonton pushed the thought aside.

The next morning, he refused the milk that Mother offered him.

"I'm fasting," he said, and went off to the synagogue with his father.

All through the morning K'tonton stood on the arm of Father's bench and prayed with the congregation. He swayed, he joined in the responses; he beat his chest at each verse of the confession. When they came to the part, "For the sin which I have committed before You in wronging a neighbor," he beat his chest especially hard.

The morning service was over.

"Go home now and eat, K'tonton," Father said. "See, your friend Sammy has eaten, and he is older than you."

K'tonton shook his head.

When the *Musaf* service was over, Mother said, "K'tonton, go home at once. You will feel sick if you fast any longer. David will take you. I have left your dinner on the table."

"Come on, K'tonton," urged his friend, David.

K'tonton was tempted. He thought of the fresh *hallah,* of the little fish ball that Mother had made especially for him, of the cool milk. But the thought of milk brought the kitten to mind. *Because of my sin, the poor kitten has no milk*, he remembered.

"Please, please, Father, let me fast. I must!" begged K'tonton.

He spoke so earnestly, Father didn't have the heart to insist.

On and on went the service. David had gone home to eat and had returned for *Neilah*, the last service of Yom Kippur. K'tonton felt odd and shaky. So this was what it was like to be hungry! Maybe this was how the kitten felt.

Maybe it was standing in the doorway now, all weak and empty. K'tonton could hear its sad *meow*. He raised his voice higher in prayer, but the voice inside whispered:

Foolish K'tonton, so what if you don't have your milk? That won't give the kitten its milk. Go and tell the truth to your mother.

K'tonton could stand it no longer. He clutched the fringe of Father's *tallit*.

"Father, Father," he called, "I must speak to Mother at once!"

Father looked down, startled. "K'tonton, little son, what is wrong? Are you sick?"

"No, no," said K'tonton, and he sobbed out the whole story!

Later that night, after the last Yom Kippur service and the final blast of the *shofar*, K'tonton stood in the kitchen watching the thin gray-and-white kitten lapping up its milk. In and out, in and out went the little pink tongue.

"Kitten, will you forgive me?" asked K'tonton soberly.

Meow, meow! said the kitten, and K'tonton knew he was forgiven.

Glossary

Rosh Hashanah——The Jewish New Year, also called the Day of Atonement, beginning a ten-day process of self-examination for sins we may have committed over the past year.

Yom Kippur——The Day of Atonement, following ten days after Rosh Hashanah, when God seals our fate for the coming year. It is a solemn day of fasting, prayer, and reflection.

Minhah——The afternoon service, one of three daily services of the Jewish liturgy.

Kol Nidre——The introductory prayer recited on the evening of Yom Kippur, annulling all vows concerning ourselves made during the course of the year.

yeshivot——Schools devoted to traditional Jewish education.

Musaf——An additional service recited on Sabbath and holidays after the morning service, following the reading of the Torah.

hallah——A loaf of bread eaten on the Sabbath and holidays. Usually braided, it is often baked in the shape of a crown for holiday meals.

Neilah——The concluding service at the climax of the Day of Atonement, during which the "gates of heaven" are said to close, and God seals our fate for the coming year. It is concluded with a blast of the shofar.

shofar——The horn of a ram or wild goat, blown on Rosh Hashanah and Yom Kippur as well as throughout the month of Elul, to stir Jews to repentance.

tallit——The prayer shawl with fringes at each corner, worn by Jews in the synagogue.

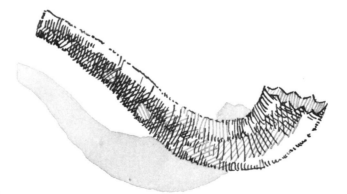